THE LAST WAY

THE LAST WAY

Cameron L. Mitchell

QUERENCIA

Querencia Press – Chicago IL

QUERENCIA PRESS

ISBN 978 1 963943 29 0

.

www.querenciapress.com

First Published in 2025

Querencia Press, LLC
Chicago IL

Printed & Bound in the United States of America

for R;

for M, M, B, and S

~~Before~~

There are countless ways to kill someone, and each way comes with its own set of risks. Do you care about getting caught? Is the chosen method sufficient for the job? If, for instance, you choose death by rock, are you willing to slam that rock against their head, harder and harder, until you're sure they're actually dead? The first blow might not be enough, after all. It could take two, three, or four more tries before they finally succumb to the violence unleashed by your hand. Can you stomach the blood, the mangled flesh, the slick and slimy things you're most certain to see? Will your stamina hold out as the victim looks up from the ground, begging you for mercy? Have you considered all the ways it might go wrong, and are you willing to do whatever it takes to finish the job when the time comes?

I've put a lot of thought into this—carefully considering the limitless ways to kill a man. The victim in this case being my father. I have killed him five, ten, fifteen times over, only to wake the next morning to the great disappointment of finding him still alive. And then, the process starts all over again. This is my life. The daily acts of violence go unfulfilled, the murder plays out in my head so many times it feels real enough to give me hope.

I have wanted him dead for so long it's hard to think of anything else. I go outside, I try to escape, but this dark desire follows me like a cloud, blocking out the sun. I exist in shadows, shivering and alone. I can't see through the storm hovering overhead. The hate inside is all-consuming like the worst kind of cancer, growing larger and stronger as it feeds on the healthy parts. It's a living thing, so palpable I can feel it lurking around each and every dark corner, waiting to sneak up behind me, to blow its warm, rancid breath against the back of my neck. It's a question of when, not if. It's the only answer I have to offer.

I've never wanted anything more. Not long from now the moment will come when his body lies before me, cold and still at last. Only then will I be able to rest, when I'm standing over him, knowing it's done. That he's gone. His very existence fills me with a rage that's sometimes frightening. Right now, the fact that he continues to breathe at all is almost more than I can bear. I may be a child, but you should know how serious I am. By the end of this, it will be done.

And, just in case you're wondering, he deserves it.

***

Time to meet my father. Here he is in the morning, awakened once again by an uncontrollable coughing fit. At times, he coughs so much I think he's on the verge of death, but of course he lives on, day after day. Slow and unsteady on his feet, he drags himself across the hallway to the bathroom, bending over the sink as he hacks up a sticky wad of phlegm that he won't even bother trying to wash away. He's a heavy smoker. The coughing is at its worst in the morning, like it's been building up in his filthy lungs all night long, waiting for release. A pack of Marlboros rarely lasts him a day—two at the most. He buys them by the carton. His smoking is just one of the many things I hate about him. I hate the flip-top boxes the cigarettes come in, the way he tap, tap, taps that first one out. I hate the dozens of discarded butts he leaves all over the house; we find them in crushed beer cans, in overflowing ashtrays he can't be bothered to empty, and in Styrofoam cups half-filled with dingy water. I hate the smoke most of all. He breathes it in slowly, taking his time as he blows it out again, making the haze hovering over our living room even thicker. The stink sticks to the curtains and fabric of the couch; the smell lingers in every corner of our house. The smoke flows from his lungs to mine, keeping us connected. Father and son. I don't want to share anything with him, but here we are breathing the same foul air. I try to avoid it by shutting my door and opening the window, but it always seeps in. When I take a break outside, the smoke is often worse upon my return, so thick it stings my eyes. I turn on the ceiling fan, I turn on the box fan in the window too, I push open another window, I open all the windows, but nothing works. The smoke still gets inside. *He* still gets inside. The stench is eternal, the stain too deep to ever wash away.

Taking up his nasty smoking habit is something I will never do. Though, I didn't always feel so strongly. Once, when I was smaller, he handed me his cigarette and told me to go put it out for him. It was a game. He wanted to see how I'd respond. He pretended to look away, going back to his conversation with Wade, one of his lowlife friends, but he kept his eye on me as I scurried off. I could feel him watching, yet he didn't try to stop me. I took the still-lit cigarette to the back of the house and made my way inside the crawlspace. The cold, hard dirt floor has a few torn plastic tarps covering it in places; the ceiling isn't tall enough for me to fully stand—not even then, when I was much smaller. In the dark, I placed my lips where his had just been and took a small puff. A part of me wanted to be like him, I suppose. I didn't know any better. Not yet. I sucked the smoke in and coughed it right back out. I coughed and coughed, struggling to catch my breath. Outside, I heard him laughing like it was some sort of joke. Like I was some sort of joke. Like he found it hilarious that I didn't know what I was doing. Me, tiny and towheaded, trying to be a big boy. As soon as I left the crawlspace, he called me over. *You're gonna be just like me, sonny boy*, he teased. And I wanted to scream, *I'll never be like you!*

I have wanted to scream so many things over the course of my short, insignificant life, but I hold it in, burying it deep in the pit of my stomach, hoping it will disappear.

It doesn't disappear, it doesn't fade into something more manageable as the days go by, each one hardly distinguishable from the next. Instead, it grows, expanding at such a rate I'm bound to lose control. Without realizing what I'm doing, I find my hands gripping my stomach, like I might stop the pain by squeezing hard enough. The pressure builds, keeping me awake through long, unrelenting nights. One of these days, it's bound to explode. I can see it now, a body blowing up from within. Eyes bulging out, limbs flying through the air. A body disassembled, split down the middle. Nothing identifiable as a boy will remain.

But let's get back to my father. He leans over the sink, still coughing uncontrollably, hacking up the poison he gleefully ingests. He is naked but for a pair of piss-stained white briefs that hang loosely on his hips; they're old and ragged with a hole torn in the back, but he never throws anything away. His legs and torso are bone-white from a lack of exposure to sun; his arms, face, and the back of his neck have darkened to a deep, rusty brown with the inverse. He's outside a lot, mowing the lawn, feeding the chickens, slopping the hog, tending the cows, working our small garden. No matter how hot and sticky it gets in the heat of our summers here in the South, he never removes his shirt. He wouldn't dream of it. I wonder if it's modesty, which seems so unlike him. He stomps through the house, loud and unabashed, burping and farting without a hint of embarrassment. He can really fill the space around him, often without uttering a single word. He doesn't seem to care what anyone thinks. Or, maybe that's just the way he is with us, his family. There are so many things about my father that I'll never know or understand. Even if I wasn't planning on killing him, it's not like he's the type to share his innermost thoughts.

Most days, he dresses the same way: a faded black t-shirt, an old pair of blue jeans that haven't been washed in ages, and his steel-toed boots—the kind made from real snakeskin. The texture of his boots is rough against my fingertips while the steel caps are smooth and always cool to the touch. Sneakers or loafers would be more comfortable, but the idea of him wearing casual shoes is preposterous—he doesn't own any. Just a couple pairs of his beloved boots, one snakeskin, the other leather. His feet stink. He refuses to change socks daily, instead wearing the same ones for an entire week. To top it off, he only bathes once a week. He grew up dirt-poor and had to use an actual outhouse when he was a young boy. He complains that we waste too much water, but, as far as I can tell, we have plenty. We certainly have enough for him to shower more frequently. But, these are his habits, too deeply ingrained for him to ever change.

He is tall and lanky with little fat to be seen other than the potbelly that protrudes more as the years pass. At the sink, he coughs his last cough and spits his last phlegm-wad before stepping over to the toilet. He kicks the lid up with his foot and unleashes a long stream of piss into the cold ceramic bowl. He shakes off the last few drops and tucks himself back inside his stained briefs. My room is directly across from the bathroom. On his way out, he turns and catches my eye. Something changes for a moment as he gazes over at me—a shadow falls over his hazel eyes, making them suddenly dark. He gropes himself suggestively and sneers at me—or maybe it's a snarl. I see that long yellow tooth at the corner of his mouth, hanging down like a fang. I turn away from him, wishing I could run away, as far as my feet would take me. To leave all this behind and never look back would be harder to achieve than what I have planned. What would I do out there, alone? And who would take care of my mother? Sitting on the bed, hands folded across my lap, I think about the way my father laughs at me less and sneers at me more.

It's not just me. These days, he laughs less in general, stretching his silences out for so long we can't help but feel their power. The long, drawn-out silences are like a bomb waiting to go off. We count down the seconds, we wait for the explosion. We squirm around, we worry, we cross our fingers and pray to a god we don't believe in that today will somehow be different. We pray for so many things but don't actually believe anyone is listening. It's a way to pass the time.

We should really know better by now. He'll never stop, not on his own. That's why I must act.

This is my father. It starts and ends with him. Dad, Daddy, Father, Papa—all the ways to name him feel too intimate, too normal. Too suggestive of a life that doesn't exist. There's a scream inside, waiting to be heard, and I can't hold it back much longer.

This is my life.

CHAPTER ONE

I wake up knowing that today is the day.

I have the perfect place to commit the perfect crime: the rock playhouse. That's what I call it—this large, natural structure in the woods made up of boulders both big and small. They stick out from the ground along the mountainside behind our house. Shrouded in the shadows of all the trees, the rock playhouse is the number one best place to get away—from myself, from life in the red house down below. The massive outcrop of rocks forms a house-like structure that looks like it was put in place by a hand reaching down from above, too large and strong to belong to a mere mortal man. It's my discovery, or so I like to think. The largest boulder rises from the ground at an angle; from below, it juts out far enough to provide shelter from the rain. The top works as a second story of sorts—or a roof I can stand upon to gaze out. Below the large, top boulder are smaller, more jagged stones sticking out from the ground. I use the sizeable dirt space between the larger rock and the smaller ones as my main living quarters. The sharper stones in front are so tall the space inside feels closed off, private. I don't have stairs to reach the second floor, but the climb isn't so bad; there's a path off to the side, and I even have a thick brown vine to grasp as I carefully make my way up. On top, it's mostly smooth and flat, but one must be careful. If you get too close to the edge, there's nothing keeping you from going over should you accidentally slip and fall. A simple misstep is all it takes, and a fall could do serious damage. Break a few bones, break your back, break your neck. The hard, jagged stones below certainly wouldn't break your fall. They'd break *you*, and it might be enough to do the job—to kill you.

That's what I'm hoping for, anyway.

I spend as much time at the rock playhouse as possible. I know the woods beyond our house better than anyone, better than I know myself even. The various paths, the rugged terrain once you clear the pasture, the best trees for climbing, for hiding—this land feels like an extension of my own self. I have walked every single inch of our mountainside forest. It remains cool in the shade even on the hottest days of summer, and there's always something new to discover. Thick, tendrilled vines hang from the trees, waiting for me to grab and take off, swinging like a primitive being from another time, like someone who belongs elsewhere, far from these mountains I call home. Once, I swung so high I thought I might take off and keep going, flying through the trees to touch that wide blue sky sparkling between the branches. I felt freer than I've ever been, but then the vine in my hands suddenly snapped, sending me crashing back to the ground below. I landed so hard it took my breath away. I didn't break anything, but my backside was sore and bruised for days.

The rock playhouse is my favorite place in the world. When I was little, I played silly games, but these days I use it more as a place to plan. So peaceful and quiet, it's the perfect haven for thinking. Often, the only noise comes from the birds chirping in the trees around me. I like pretending the playhouse is all mine, that I live there on my own, completely alone.

Maybe I'll make friends one day and invite them over. In the meantime, I manage to keep busy. I spend hours reading books borrowed from the library. I jot down words I like in my notebook. Words like *precipice*. I think of how I might use it in a sentence: *My father tripped and tumbled over the sharp* precipice, *falling to his bloody death below*. I sometimes write the sentences down, along with other thoughts. If I'm inspired, I draw pictures of the trees around me, or faces of people I don't know. I create new worlds and map them out. I think of all the things I'll do one day when I'm really on my own. I relax, far from the sound of my father's boots stomping across the creaky floor. I try not to think about the long silences waiting to be filled by whatever comes next. I go off to the side to pee, far enough away from the main structure to keep it from getting stinky. I watch the urine splash against the dirt and run down the mountain in a little stream towards my real home, the red house. Shaking off the last drops, I wonder if I could use leaves as toilet paper if I had to. I've never tried, but I'm also never in the woods *that* long. I always return to the red house by dark. It makes me laugh, the idea of using leaves as toilet paper.

It's Saturday, and I'm up earlier than my father. On weekends, he likes to sleep in. I used to watch Saturday morning cartoons, keeping the volume low so I wouldn't wake him. Sitting so close to the screen, I probably damaged my eyesight, but it's the only way I could hear. I no longer spend Saturday mornings watching cartoons. With everything going on, it's hard to take the world of bright colors and happy endings seriously.

During the week, my father wakes before me. He works construction and must get to the site early. The only thing he leaves behind is a freshly smashed cigarette butt and the smell of smoke still lingering in the air—proof he was here. There are the dishes used to make his breakfast, piled up in the sink. He always has the same thing: two fried eggs, a few slices of bacon, toast with butter, and coffee. Mother offers to fry me up something as well, but I usually enjoy a bowl of cold cereal instead.

I creep through the house with little cat feet, biding my time. In the kitchen, I prepare my cereal and sit at the table, thinking. This is my time to plan, to plot his death, to carefully work out the details so nothing goes wrong. I'll go up to the woods before he and my mother get out of bed. I'll spend time at the rock playhouse, maybe an hour or so. Then, I'll return with news of an injured animal—a deer, shot by some idiot hunter who must have crossed onto our land as he tracked it down. I'll rehearse the story until I'm sure it's convincing, and then I'll carry the lie back down to the red house. With the fervor of a normal child, I'll tell my father about the deer I found—the blood soaking its fur, the way it can still lift its head, just barely. The poor, wounded animal. I'll emphasize that someone must have intruded upon our land to shoot the deer, but they didn't finish the job. They left the animal to suffer.

The idea of a trespasser will drive my father crazy. He'll hate the thought of a perfect stranger not only intruding where he doesn't belong but also leaving such a mess behind. Feeling duty-bound, he'll do what needs to be done. That's the way he is with things that belong to him. He must look after his kingdom, keeping everything in perfect order.

I finish my cereal, rinse the bowl, gulp down a glass of water, and then head outside. I make my way up to the electric fence and slide beneath it, keeping an eye on the cows nearby. They don't usually bother me, but I'm careful, just in case. We used to have a bull, and he was one hell of a holy terror. He once broke out and destroyed my swing set with his horns, enraged at everything in his path as he charged through the yard. It took my father and his friend Wade forever to get the beast back into the pasture, safely enclosed behind the electric fence.

Thinking of my devious plan and how today will be the day, I start skipping along, happy as I've ever been. Soon, I'm at the edge of the woods. I turn around to look down at the red house. My father is in there, probably waking right about now. I bet he's coughing and spitting and moaning about his aching back. Feeling brave, I stretch my arm out and flip up my middle finger, aiming it at the red house. Today, I am brave. I am strong enough to do what must be done.

After crossing into the woods, I slow my pace, trying to kill a little time. I don't actually need to visit the rock playhouse for my plan to work. But all this waiting around is killing me. For my entire life, I've done nothing but wait. And now, something big is about to happen. I tell myself to be patient, I breathe in and out, slowly. I close my eyes and count to 100, speeding through the numbers in my head even as I keep telling myself to go slow. When I open my eyes again, I start the count all over as I hobble around in a circle.

Time passes, but not fast enough, so I start walking up to the rock playhouse after all, rehearsing my story to make sure I get it right. I saw something moving nearby, a large shape, and when I got closer, I realized it was a deer, obviously wounded or else it would have hopped up and ran away. A dark wetness covered its fur—blood, obviously blood. A lot of it. Clearly a gunshot wound, but who would have been hunting on our land? I repeat the details over and over again, adding more each time. Trying to figure out what works, what sounds most believable. The deer, the poor deer, its fur matted with dirt and leaves, its belly black with blood. The way it growled at me, baring its teeth—teeth covered in dark streaks of blood still glistening. The noises it made, sounds I won't soon forget: low grunts and weakening growls, a whistle and a wheeze as it struggled to breathe. The look in its eye aimed at the sky, knowing each sharp, labored breath might be its last. A failing effort to rise that resulted only in a new spurt of blood from a wound that will never heal.

By the time I reach the rock playhouse, I'm feeling more confident than ever. I'm ready, I can do this. Buzzing with anticipation, I kick one of the long, pointed rocks jutting out from the ground. I kick it again, I jump in the air, I do a little twirl, I scream as loud as I can; the booming sound of my voice echoes across the land. For the last time, I close my eyes and count to 100. When I open them, I know it's time. I begin my descent, racing down through the woods, skipping over stones and branches, no amount of speed's enough. Finally, I reach the edge of the woods and emerge fully transformed, like a newborn thing. With the powerful heat of physical endurance coursing through me, I feel capable of anything. I'm aware of my body in a way I haven't been before, each and every part. The pathetic weak little boy that I once was is now gone, and I'll never look back. Overcome with excitement, I almost forget to duck when I reach the electric fence. I throw myself down at the very last second and tumble beneath the single line of barbed wire—I feel like the hero, facing impossible feats, ready to save the day. Rising, I take a moment to catch my breath and see a large grass stain on the side of my shorts. At least I didn't get electrocuted.

Down at the house, I find him in the living room, sitting in silence with a cigarette. I brace myself before drawing closer to tell him about the wounded deer. In one long spiel that leaves me breathless by the time I get it all out, I describe the scene. The dark blood soaking the animal's fur. The awful sounds it made while just barely managing to lift its head, staring at me with the saddest brown eyes I've ever seen. The poor thing, it was so scared, and I—I didn't know what to do. Someone, they must have shot it, and now it's there, on our land left to suffer.

Though he says nothing at first, I can tell it's working. I detect a hint of suspicion in his eyes, however, and know what he must be thinking. He's wondering why I'm so excited, why I'm talking to him at all since I usually avoid him at all costs. I look away as if I've suddenly lost interest, reciting the next part with less enthusiasm. "Probably some hunter," I mumble, "trespassing again."

He leans forward to smash his cigarette out in the ashtray. "Bring me my boots," he says. He hasn't asked me to grab his boots in a long time, but I do as I'm told, like a good son. I follow *his* lead. I let him believe he's the one calling the shots.

By the time I return, he's opening the gun cabinet. I gasp, nearly dropping the boots. I hate guns. They're so loud, so explosive, and they have the power to end everything with a single pull of the trigger. The deep black darkness inside the barrel of a gun is a void waiting to draw you inside. Though I do know how to use one if I have to—*he* taught me how. Guns are not toys, he claims, though he has used them to play games. Games to keep us in line, games that make sure we know who's boss.

I should have developed a better plan since guns make me so nervous, but it's too late to back out now. There's no way for this to work without a gun being involved. How else would he finish off the wounded animal—the deer that doesn't really exist. What did I think was going to happen? I clench my fists and tap my foot up and down nervously, upset at my oversight.

He props the rifle against the gun cabinet and shoves a few cartridges in his pocket. Sitting down again, he stares at me, waiting, so I hand the boots over. He yanks his stinky socks out from inside the boots and pulls them on. The big toe on his right foot pokes out through a large hole in the sock. He's got less raggedy socks but hardly ever throws anything away. With his boots on, he grabs his cigarettes and hauls the rifle over his shoulder, heading outside. I rush to catch up. By the time I reach him, he's already lighting a cigarette. He glances down at me briefly, looking annoyed. I race around him, walking faster. As we make our way across the pasture and into the woods, I find myself easily outpacing him. I know this land better than he ever will, and I don't have his pack-a-day habit or bad back to slow me down. I'm also smaller and more agile, making it much easier to find the quickest way through a tangle of vines or thick brush. He slows even more as the incline increases. Short of breath, he starts coughing and spitting. I turn to watch him smash his cigarette out against the side of a tree before tossing it away. *Hope you enjoyed it*, I think, hiding my smirk. *It'll be your last.*

As we approach the rock playhouse, my whole body tenses up. It's hard to believe the biggest, most significant moment of my life is upon us. He starts asking where the deer is, looking around. "Just up there," I tell him. "Not too far." I quickly scramble up the side of the playhouse to the top. He struggles to follow. His cowboy boots aren't good for the steepness of these woods. He's almost lost his footing a few times already, making him cranky as hell. At the top, I wait, my muscles tightening so much they hurt.

When he finally makes it up, he grips his knee with one hand and hunches over to catch his breath. He looks around for the deer and asks where it is. I point over to the edge of the rock, near some tall brush off to the side. "It's right over there," I tell him. "Don't you see it?" Slowly, he draws closer to the edge. After one, two, three more steps, I know it's time. I take a deep breath and close my eyes. When I open them, the world is still and silent, and my mind is mostly empty. I take off, running to him, my father, and push as hard as I can. My surprise attack works. He lurches forward, tumbling over the edge. The gun flies into the air, landing out of reach but nearby. I move without thinking, inching closer to the edge. I can't see him, I can't hear him, but I know he's down there. Not a wounded deer, but a dead dad. I'm scared at first but also relieved that it's finally over.

And then sound returns to the world. The birds chirping, the light rustle of a breeze blowing through.

Something is wrong. It takes me a moment to realize I am holding my breath for no reason. The world shifts around me as I start to breathe again. Inching even closer to the edge, I get down on my hands and knees and force myself to look over. There I find him at the bottom, his body twisted at odd angles amidst jagged stones lining the front of my playhouse. He lies perfectly still, a small trickle of blood runs down the side of his mouth. I feel dizzy for a moment, like I might fall over the edge to join him, so I push myself back, desperately crawling away from the danger.

Standing, I brush the dirt from my hands and knees and make my way over to the side of the playhouse, rushing halfway down the slope. Before getting too close, I stop short. Something horrible happens, something I knew could be a possibility. The body moves, just a little at first. An awful groan escapes his lips as he raises his head. I gaze down at the body and realize the job isn't done. Through half-closed eyes, he stares at me, scared and confused. I have never seen him like this, so weak and vulnerable. He's wounded but not dead, just like the deer I lied about.

A wave suddenly washes over me, returning me to the job that needs to be done, to the world that will continue spinning long after I'm gone. I glance around frantically, scanning the ground for the right implement. Just a few feet away, I find it, the weapon that will bring the destruction I crave. I pick up the rock, and it's just the right size, fitting so perfectly in my hand I can hardly believe my luck. I hold it tight, feeling the weight of its power in my hand. Carefully, I make my way down the embankment without slipping and falling. I am nimble, quick. I can do this. Drawing closer to the body, I tell myself that it's just that and nothing more. A body so bruised and broken it's crying out to be finished off. It's begging for mercy, the mercy to end all suffering. It's going to be a mess, all the blood splashing out, the shards of bone and meaty bits of flesh flying into the air. It's already a crime scene, so I might as well get on with it. I am a criminal, after all. Will they know I'm also a hero who's finally saved the day? I lift up the heavy stone and hold it high above my head.

CHAPTER TWO

Or, there's another way. A slight variation. Everything the same but for a few important changes. The wounded deer. The hunter who invaded our land and shot the animal, leaving it sprawled across the ground, bleeding out. Alive, but suffering. The intruder hearing me approach, not wanting to get caught trespassing, so he made his escape without finishing what he started. Scrambling off like a coward, he left the dirty work for someone else. My father is the only one who can clean up the mess. Once he knows about it, he'll agree—he'll insist on taking care of the problem himself. My father, protector of the red house that is our home and all the land that surrounds it, the land he's proud to call his own after growing up dirt-poor *without a pot to piss in*, as he's so fond of saying. My father, king of the castle—*his* castle, not ours. This land, his. My bedroom is not mine, my comics are not mine, my notebooks filled with my notes and my drawings are not really mine.

Mine, he's told me more than once, squeezing my face with his big bear paw, making me look at all the things I always thought belonged to me. *Say it.*

Yours, yours, it's all yours, I'd agree, trying to squirm away from his grasp.

Everything, his. We mustn't forget.

Sometimes, I stare at my hands, wondering if they're actually mine. I stare for so long I forget where I am, what I'm doing. I forget who I am, even. I'm not sure I ever knew.

As I tell him about the wounded deer, I remember who he is, I remember everything he's done. I don't make eye contact—I wouldn't dare. I glance off to the side, I mumble, I pretend to be reporting what I've seen out of a sense of duty. Me, a good soldier. A good son. I'm good at pretending. Pretend there's nothing wrong, pretend you're not scared, pretend your heart isn't full of hate. I've pretended so many things. Pretending is lying, but I like to think of it more as telling a story. It's usually harmless, though not today. Not for him.

My father listens to everything I have to say. It's hard to know what he's thinking since he's good at pretending too. "Bring me my boots," he says at last, and I'm relieved my plan is working. I remember to keep my face rigid and blank. I can't let him see the excitement threatening to bubble up. I am mopey, I am quiet, I am still the same son he's come to expect. As far as he's concerned, there will be no surprises. All is well in his kingdom, almost. He just has to take care of this one little thing with the deer.

I bring him his boots and watch him retrieve the gun from the tall cabinet in the corner. Its door has a large glass panel to put the weapons on display, to show them off, but he keeps the glass covered with an old towel for some reason, hiding what's inside. Maybe it's better this way, so we can pretend there's nothing to fear. Or maybe it's worse. We know they're there, locked inside the cabinet, waiting. The guns. The cartridges. The long, smooth barrels ready to explode. We can pretend we don't know what's hidden inside, but, of course, we always know.

And I should have known from the start that a gun had to be a part of my plan for it to work. A rifle in this case, perfect to kill a deer.

Perfect to kill a man.

I lead the way up through the yard, across the pasture, and into the woods. He smokes, he coughs, he spits, he leans against a tree for support. He is stronger than me, I know, but I have my advantages. I am small and agile and could easily outrun him. Unlike his own, filthy rotten from years of smoking, my lungs can take this fresh mountain air in deep and breathe it back out, slowly.

At the rock playhouse, I turn around, hoping he feels ashamed that he can't keep up. I point to the top of the playhouse, telling him it's there. I offer to hold the gun while he makes his way up the steep incline. He hands it over easily enough, not giving it a second thought, and I hold the weapon tight, feeling the weight of its power in my hands. "Use the vine," I tell him. In this strange reversal of roles, I am the one who knows best. "It's easy, just pull yourself up." I watch him from behind, struggling to keep his footing. The boots make his climb harder. The boots make most things that take place outside harder, but he wears them anyway, day after day, forever set in his ways. We would never tell him he's wrong. We mustn't speak up, no matter what. It makes everything worse.

Suddenly, I think back to the last time he dyed his hair black in the bathroom. This rugged macho man with a towel draped around his shoulders, too vain to accept the gray that's coming in on both sides of his head, right above his ears, reminding him that he won't live forever after all. He slammed the door in my face when he caught me staring.

I take a deep breath and hold it, I switch the safety off, and I lift the rifle up, taking aim. I feel like a coward for doing it this way, with his back turned to me, completely unaware of what's about to happen. But there are worse things in the world than being a coward.

I put my finger on the trigger. Careful now, I take my time, waiting for the perfect moment.

~~LAST NIGHT~~

Last night, I stood at the kitchen counter helping my mother with the dishes. She washed our dirty cups, forks and spoons, plates, bowls, pots, and pans before handing them over for me to rinse. She took her time, scrubbing each item more thoroughly than usual. When I accidentally banged a pot against the sink, she put a hand on my arm and gently squeezed. I understood, of course. She was telling me to be more careful, warning me not to make too much noise. With a small towel, I dried off the larger items, putting them back in place where they belonged, some in the cabinets below the sink, others in the ones above. I left the cups, plates, and silverware in the rack to dry. In the living room, the television droned on quietly. Cigarette smoke drifted through the air, circling us in its haze. Suddenly, we sensed movement in the other room, and then the recliner groaned with a sharp creak. The noise of the television disappeared, leaving behind a silence waiting to be filled. My mother stopped what she was doing, holding perfectly still. Holding her breath, just like me.

At the sound of his boots hitting the floor behind us, we both flinched, afraid of what might be coming next.

CHAPTER THREE

I wake up knowing that today is the day.

I close my bedroom door, but not all the way. Completely shutting it would attract unnecessary attention. Privacy isn't allowed in the little red house. He knows all, he sees all. Like an evil god. I try to carve out places of my own. The closet in my room juts out, creating a small alcove. The head of my twin bed is tucked inside that alcove. The narrow space between the bed and the wall of the alcove is hidden from view of anyone who happens to walk by, making it my own private space. If anyone should approach my bedroom door, I'll hear the sound of their steps before they appear and have plenty of time to hide what mustn't be revealed. This spot in the alcove is the perfect place to plan my father's most untimely death.

Today, I am a chemist with a steady hand—I am a mad scientist with a perfect plan. Feeling mischievous, I rub my palms together, reveling in the wickedness of what I'm about to do. He'll never see it coming. If all goes well, it'll be over before he can stop it.

Actually, I prefer chemist to mad scientist. I'm not the one who's mad, after all. I am angry, it's true, and have been for so long I can hardly remember anything else, but I am not mad. I am a man of science with precise, measured moves; my hands are capable of remaining steady no matter what. They will not tremble in fear. Of course,

I understand that I am nothing but a boy with very little power, but I can feel a new strength in these unflinching hands of mine and take a moment to admire them.

They have already done most of the hard work. There's a long white scar across my left hand; it starts between my thumb and index finger but takes a sudden turn to cross the top of my wrist, like someone tried to cut me open with a jagged knife that suddenly slipped. Gazing further down along my arm, I can see faded yellow bruises that remind me of something putrid. But I can't think of those mysterious marks right now. I have a job to do.

I take a deep breath and close my eyes; when I open them, I'm able to focus my full attention on the task at hand. I pull the plastic sandwich bag from beneath my mattress; it holds my supply of crushed sleeping pills. Cradling it in one hand as I lift it up and down, testing the weight of my supply, I wonder if it's enough. I need more than I've ever used before. I'm not just putting him to sleep for the evening like I've done in the past. I'm putting him to sleep for good this time.

The baggie's quite full, but I can't take any chances. Although I've assumed the role of chemist, I have no idea how many sleeping pills it takes to kill a man. Fifteen? Twenty? I've heard of people swallowing a bottle of sleeping pills when they want to off themselves, so that's a good place to start. There's at least a bottle's worth of crushed pills inside the bag already, and I have an unopened one to work with as well. But as I think back to all the times I've drugged my father over the past year or so, I remember the constant fear that he'd notice something was off if I poured too much of the white powder into his drink. Before, I only wanted to knock him out for the night so he'd leave us alone. And it worked. Finally, I found something that worked! He fell asleep on the couch much earlier than normal and never noticed a thing. By the time he woke the next morning, he didn't suspect anything out of the ordinary had occurred the night before. If he had a headache or felt groggy, he blamed the booze. He had no idea what I'd done because I was so careful, slipping only small amounts into his drink at a time when he went to the bathroom, quickly stirring it around with my finger before he got back. The first time, I basically held my breath until he fell asleep, terrified he might notice what I'd done. What if the pills made his whiskey taste different? Or might he notice a slight discoloration in the amber liquid?

But it worked out just fine. By the third time, my confidence had increased, so I poured more into his drink, making sure he'd pass out even faster. Once, I accidentally spilled more than I meant to inside his cup and panicked when I couldn't make it dissolve fast enough. Even then, when he took a sip, he didn't notice a thing. That night, I wondered if I might have accidentally killed the bastard; secretly, I hoped that I had. Yet, to my great disappointment, he woke the following morning. Coughing and spitting from all the smoking but still very much alive.

I've also drugged his cans of beer, which is trickier in some ways but easier in others. Getting the rocky powder inside without leaving a trace is more challenging since the opening of the can is so much smaller, but once it's in, I just shake the beer around, doing my best to make sure the substance dissolves. It doesn't matter if the beer suddenly looks a little cloudy since he'll never see it.

I take one of the hardcover books from the closet and turn it over. It's the latest Stephen King novel. My mom buys books like this for us to read when she can. I get to go first, mostly because it takes her longer to finish. Unlike me, she doesn't have a lot of free time to spend reading. We keep the books hidden in my closet since my father doesn't approve of such frivolous purchases, insisting they're a waste of money. I've never seen him taking the time to read anything. The idea of catching him curled up with a book on the couch is absurd. It'd be like staring into the sky and catching sight of two moons. He gets irritated whenever we talk about our favorite books, so we try not to in his presence. Sometimes, I think he hates anything that makes us happy.

After sliding the dust jacket off and setting it aside, I place the book on the floor in the corner of the alcove. Here, no one can see it from the doorway. I pour some pills on the book and start crushing them with the smooth rock I found in the creek bed. It's the perfect size for the job—not *too* large to be cumbersome, though big enough to do the job. I'm able to quietly grind the pills down and sweep the rocky dust into the sandwich bag. Once I've crushed ten more pills and added them to my supply, I blow the dust off the rock, I wipe the book clean and put it away, and I seal the bag, shoving it under my pillow so I can easily retrieve it when the time is right.

Now, I wait.

Most of my life is spent waiting, watching, and listening for signs of what might be coming next. Always being on guard gets exhausting.

In the meantime…in the meantime, what? I turn to the blank pages of my notebook and start jotting down whatever comes to mind—

In the meantime.

In the *mean* time, I prove that I am crafty, I prove that I am cruel. Or, at least I can be. I will be. This time, when it counts the most, I will show no mercy.

In the *me* time, I suddenly have doubts. I stare at my hands, wondering if they're capable of doing what I need them to do. They've taken me this far, but is it far enough? Here I am, alone with these thoughts and notions, these plans and solutions. Here I am, alone, counting down the seconds, minutes, hours until I know the time is right. Here I am, hoping there's enough time. To get through this, to survive. But is the time I need even mine? Like everything else, I fear it belongs to him too. Time itself. His schedule, his rules, his everything.

Nothing else matters.

I slam my notebook shut and throw it across the room, tired of trying to figure out a riddle that can't be solved. Glancing down, I catch sight of a large oval bruise on my inner arm, right across my bicep. It's different from the others, the ones that have mostly faded. I can't remember where all these bruises come from. They start as deep, dark stains that slowly turn pale and sallow, fading until nothing's left. My mother says I'm clumsy, always tripping over something. My father—he doesn't say anything about them at all.

I bring my arm closer to my face, discovering that the dark oval mark fits the shape of my mouth. Now I remember—first there were bite marks, then the bruise. It was something I had to do. An irresistible urge. Like so many other things, it wasn't a decision I made. It just happened. I put my mouth to my arm and bit down hard, so hard it should have hurt more. With my own teeth, I nearly broke the skin, but I had to do it to keep the scream inside from finding its way out. There was a deeper pain, one that's always there. To forget that other pain, I bit down as hard as I could. Biting is better than screaming, and it worked. For a while, it worked.

Other bruises come and go, but this one I will remember.

A sudden movement at the far end of the house sends vibrations across the floor and through the walls—something rises, emerging from the dark. I feel unsteady and lightheaded, like an earthquake has shaken me loose, but I tell myself we don't get earthquakes here in the mountains, that we are safe from that, at least. But then I remember that my father *is* an earthquake. He's the disaster waiting to destroy us all.

It's him moving at the far end of the house, making his way to the kitchen. This could be it, the moment I've been waiting for. I snap out of it, breaking through the cloud that threatens to keep me in the dark. I look at the bruise one last time and jump into action. The bag of pills—my weapon of choice—is in my hand, is in my pocket. Carefully, I rise, making sure the mattress doesn't squeak. I'm in control again, *me*. This is my opportunity to change the course of our lives once and for all. I can't keep waiting for the wind to blow in a different direction. So far, these winds have done nothing but push us closer to the edge.

At the door, I pause long enough to listen carefully. His boots thump across the linoleum floor of the kitchen. For a few moments, there is silence, but then the sound of his steps returns as he heads back to the living room. The recliner groans like something dying as he falls into its musty embrace. While crossing to the bathroom, I casually glance down the hallway to see he's poured himself a cup of whiskey. I know it's whiskey because of the Styrofoam cup. He only uses those when he's drinking the hard stuff. He once kept the same dirty, white Styrofoam cup in the cabinet beside his booze for nearly a week. It started breaking down, crumbling from the alcohol. I don't know why he doesn't drink whiskey from a glass that can be washed regularly if he wants to use the same one. It's yet another thing about him I'll never understand.

Inside the bathroom, I shut the door and allow myself a little smile. I have a good feeling about this. I don't really need to pee but go through the motions anyway to make my trip to the bathroom more believable. With the tip of my foot, I lift the toilet seat and wait for what I feel is the appropriate amount of time it would take to empty my bladder before easing it back down and flushing. While washing up at the sink, I'm caught off guard by the sight of myself in the mirror. My face is pale, my eyes are gleaming with an excited fervor. For a moment, it's like someone else is standing before me, gazing out. Someone older, someone taller. Someone with similar features but who's so unlike me it sends a chill up my spine. Quickly, I bend down to splash water across my face. When I return my gaze to the mirror, whatever I saw is gone, but I can still feel its presence, waiting to reveal something I don't want to see.

I dry my face and close my eyes, focusing on what this is all about. The mission, the task. I must decide where to keep watch—the kitchen, the living room, or my bedroom? My bedroom is the obvious choice. I don't want to get too close to the target. Not yet. A flicker of doubt in my abilities to complete this gnaws at me. But I am stealthy in my moves, I have practiced the necessary steps to accomplish my goals. I can do this. In my bedroom, I can stay out of sight until the time is right. The swell of confidence returns. Without looking in the mirror again, I exit the bathroom and return to my bedroom, leaving the door wide open this time. Here, I'll wait—however long it takes.

And it doesn't take long. The sound of the recliner creaking when he gets up is a long, lonesome sigh of relief. His boots march my way, pounding across the living room and down the hall as he makes his way to the bathroom. I jump into action, armed with my bag of white powder. Keeping my ears perked and my eyes trained on the hallway, I dump about a third of the contents into his drink and quickly stir it with my finger. I panic for a moment, worried I've put too much in at one time to go unnoticed, but there's nothing I can do about it now. Slipping the bag back into my pocket, I rush to the kitchen and hear the bathroom door opening just as I reach the sink. I scrub my hands with soap to rinse the smell of whiskey away. I can't stand its strong, sharp odor. I can't stand anything about the rich, amber liquid since whiskey days are the worst.

Just as he returns to his recliner, I freeze, holding my breath. Behind me, I can hear him leaning forward to grab his cup, pausing for what feels like an eternity before taking a sip. Eventually, he sets the cup down again—I don't hear it, exactly, but I can feel it happening. I wait, I listen. When I hear the creaking of the recliner as he settles in, I'm finally able to breathe again. He has no idea what I've done! My plan is working. I pour myself a glass of water and drink it down in one long gulp.

I wonder how many more cups of whiskey he'll have, how many more trips to the bathroom he'll take, and how many more chances I'll get to finish the job. Over the course of a typical whiskey day, he has at least three or four cups, leisurely drinking them as the late afternoon turns to night. He often mixes in a beer or two as well, going back and forth between that and his drink of choice. The more he has, and the quicker he throws them back, the better chance I have of making this work. It's an odd feeling, hoping he drinks more and quicker since I've come to dread his whiskey days so much. But today is different.

Waiting for the next step, I can't help but feel impatient. Just as I'm about to leave the kitchen to return to my post in the bedroom, I hear his recliner squeaking again. He's getting up, he's coming my way. We pass each other, predator and prey—I breathe in his musky scent. Near the sink, he's retrieving a glass, and in a split second, I decide to act, though I know it's risky. As he pours himself some water, I pull my bag out and dump more powder into his drink, quickly stirring it around with my finger. I'm quick but not quick enough—just as I'm turning away from what I've done, he's suddenly before me, staring down with cold, dark eyes.

"What are you doing?" he asks.

Surprisingly, I answer at once, "My friend Bobby says his dad always drinks beer after liquor, to like chase it. Is that what you do?"

He narrows his eyes, regarding me suspiciously. If he uncovers the truth, I might be the one who dies tonight. But then, his face softens, and I know I'm ok. "Hmm," he grunts. "Ever' now and then, I reckon."

I shrug and dart back to the kitchen, thinking about how Bobby doesn't even exist. I'm not sure where I came up with that. It'd be nice to have a friend named Bobby, though. It'd be nice to have a friend.

I shake it off—the loneliness—and focus on what a good job I'm doing. Not only have I managed to sneak more powder into his drink, but I've planted a seed in his mind making him think about how refreshing a nice cold beer would taste right about now. He'll be cracking one open any minute, I'm sure.

"Hey," he calls out, "bring me a beer then."

Alright, sure, I think, smiling like a killer. *Anything you want.*

In no particular rush, I open the fridge, I pull out a cold can from the back, and I bring it to him, all while keeping my mask of indifference carefully in place. My satisfied smile is now on the inside, bright and wide. I turn away and head back to my room, listening to the hiss of his beer popping open.

As the evening wears on, he takes two more bathroom breaks, allowing me plenty of time to sneak in two more doses of white sleeping dust. The last one almost finishes the bag. In my covert maneuvering, pretending I need a snack or more water from the kitchen, I peer over at him, taking note of his increasingly drowsy eyes. He's already having a hard time keeping them open, and his breathing has slowed, more so with each passing moment.

Who's in trouble now?

We'll say he got drunk like he always gets drunk, and he might have taken some pills. Too many pills. Really, we can't say for sure. We can't even say what kind of pills he takes. We're not aware of everything he does. There are things he wouldn't want us to know about, after all. That's true for anyone. Maybe it was suicide. He's always in a bad mood. Or, it could have been an accident. Maybe he didn't mean to take so many pills but lost count in his desperate need to get a good night of sleep. Drunk people make mistakes. They do stupid things all the time. They're capable of doing awful, destructive things that hurt themselves as much as they hurt those around them.

We don't have to say anything at all. Later, when this is all over, we can say we found him unresponsive, unable to wake him. His body stiff, his skin cold and rubbery, we don't know what happened. No one knows the truth but me, and I can keep my mouth shut. I've spent a lifetime learning how to stay quiet.

For now, he's still with us, but I can tell the pills are working. He starts to get up but immediately falls back, reaching a hand up to his head, his eyes, dizzy and confused; with great effort, he tries again, making it this time, though he's so unsteady on his feet he has to close his eyes and concentrate all his energy on remaining upright. Hunching over, he licks his lips, he runs his tongue over his teeth, trying to wet his parched mouth. Slowly, he looks around the room, which must be shifting out of focus by now. He mumbles a single word I can't quite understand; he tries again, just barely getting it out: *water*. He wants water. My sad, pathetic, dying dad, desperate for a drink of water to quench the unrelenting thirst he can't quite comprehend. His mouth, so fuzzy and dry, his head filled with a fog that thickens more as the mix of pills and alcohol take full effect. He takes a step towards the kitchen but seems to be having a hard time making his body do what he wants it to do. Changing course, he wobbles over to the couch, collapsing as his body gives out. The television drones on, though I doubt he can hear it—I doubt he can hear much of anything now, not with his senses beginning to fail. He shifts around uneasily, just barely managing to throw his arm over his face, sinking into the darkness. Accepting it because he has no choice. I can almost hear the sound of his cold black heart beating slower, and slower, and slower.

I watch his every move from the doorway of my bedroom, unafraid of him catching me. Unafraid of all the usual things, I watch him fall into a sleep that won't end. For the very first time, I feel completely unafraid.

I slip into the living room, turn the television off, and sit on the floor, crossing my legs to get more comfortable. All of this will be over soon.

CHAPTER FOUR

Today is the day, the one I've been waiting for.

Walking along the back wall of the house, I run my hand across one of the long, red panels of wood. I think of this little red house we call home, recalling the time two summers ago when my father forced me to help him repaint it. *Make yourself useful for a change,* he said. So, I gripped the ladder with both hands to hold it steady as he climbed up. My role seemed pointless, but he said it was important. It'd help keep him from accidentally falling. If that happened, he might break his arm or leg. He might even break his neck, he warned.

If only, I thought.

But I held the ladder in place, giving it my all. If I failed in this one simple task, I'd be in big trouble. I didn't care if he fell and hurt himself, of course, but I didn't want to give him a reason to fly into yet another rage. When something goes wrong, someone has to pay. With sweaty palms, I held that ladder as tight as I could, growing more anxious with each step he took up the rungs. The whole time he was on the ladder, I couldn't relax or let my guard down, not even for a second. Whenever it moved at all, I tightened my grip or adjusted my stance. Should something go wrong, I had to be ready to react. With a single misstep, he could slip and fall. Things are always going wrong, I've discovered. People fall down, they have accidents, they forget to be careful. It happens all the time.

As the day wore on, I offered more assistance. I rinsed brushes out before handing them over, filled the bucket we were using with fresh water at the spigot, and scraped away large swaths of old paint all on my own. The fact that the original coat was chipping away in so many different places is what made my father decide to paint the house in the first place. We couldn't have that—our red house chipping and cracking—so we scraped off what we could and painted over the rest, making what was old new again. I enjoyed it, this work with my hands. It made me feel important, like I was contributing. Like I mattered. But I'd never let him know that, so I kept my mask of indifference on, pretending it was all such a drag.

Day has now turned to night. The dingy yellow light from the kitchen window over my head cuts into the darkness around me. I've been on both sides of this wall. I've seen my mother on the other side, alone, washing dishes. I've been on that side with her, helping out. I wonder what we look like standing side by side, viewed from the outside. Do we seem like any other mother and son, normal and unafraid?

The light spilling from the kitchen window reveals nothing. Sometimes, it's better to remain in the dark.

My father is inside the red house, and I'm here, just outside its back wall. I don't bother looking in. I don't need to. I know what's in there, and I know what's coming.

Mother has gone to church, which means she's safe. We hardly ever accompany her, and she never pushes it, not even with me. I don't think she actually cares much for all that religious talk, the myths of a higher power watching over us. We're in the midst of our own myth, afraid of how our story will end. I'm trying to change it; she's doing her best to accept it. It's hard, but getting away to church offers relief. Every now and then, she just needs a little break to make it through another day, so she volunteers to do all sorts of things. She bakes pies for potlucks, she helps with fundraisers, she takes our hand-me-downs to give to the less fortunate. She sits with the church ladies, discussing whatever it is they discuss over tall glasses of sweet tea. They gossip, I'm sure. I can hear them now, talking about that new woman who joined the congregation, the timid one with the husband who drinks too much—but then they quickly change the subject, embarrassed to have brought it up since my mother also has a husband who drinks too much. I wonder if that other husband screams and hits people when he drinks too much, like my father. I wonder if the church ladies talk about that as well, when my mother isn't around.

Or maybe they spend their time yapping about the end of the world. It's a popular topic here in the mountains, mostly amongst the old-timers. The end is coming, they say. Any day now.

They're probably right. It feels like something big is about to happen. I'm not sure it's a bad thing, this end of the world they're so worried over. It would be an end, anyway.

With my right hand, I scratch along the side of the house, scraping away tiny flecks of red paint. Some of them get stuck beneath my fingernails. The further I drag my hand, the more it hurts. I stare down at my stained fingertips, thinking back to that day I helped my father paint the house. Even then, I wanted him dead. What if I hadn't held the ladder so tightly? What if I shook it, just a little? What if I shook it harder, causing him to fall?

That would have been pointless. Our house is one-story, so a fall wouldn't be fatal. At best, he might break an arm or a leg. Still, maybe I could try again. Maybe I could tell him some shingles have blown off the roof. And then, I'd hold that ladder for him once again, watching him climb up. This time, I could strategically place a large rock on the ground for him to hit when I shake him loose—but he'd have to land on it just right. Or, maybe I could use a rock to bash his skull in after the fall, hoping no one would notice he didn't land against it on his own. Maybe I could leave something sharp and sturdy nearby, like a large pair of shears, a stake of some sort, or a rake—and maybe he'd land just right, impaling himself. Maybe I could take the sharp object and impale him myself, making it look like he fell on it.

Maybe, maybe, maybe.

I can't depend on maybe forever. So instead, I'm going to burn it all down. Everything. I've already drugged my father with a large dose of sleeping pills. I grounded them up and slipped them into his drink. He should be sprawled across the couch right about now, falling into a state of unconsciousness so deep nothing will ever wake him again. Not the sound of blank pages being ripped from my notebook and crumpled up, not the rise of smoke from the small fires I'll set all around him. He's a careless man, always drinking and smoking too much. It won't be hard to believe it was an accident. It won't take much for the ugly yellow curtains behind the couch to go up in flames. Along with the notebook pages, I'll use one of the Stephen King novels he hates us having as well, ripping the pages out and setting them ablaze in strategic places so the fire grows and grows and grows. As I retreat to the backdoor, I'll light everything I can on fire and watch the smoke spread and thicken, knowing he's breathing it deep inside his filthy lungs—lungs that must already be black with the damage of so many years' worth of cigarettes. He'll shift and stir but will be too groggy and out of it to save himself. He'll likely suffocate from all the smoke before the flames fully consume him—I wonder if he'll suffer.

Once the fire's raging out of control, I'll make my escape, fleeing up the hill, across the pasture, stopping at the edge of the woods where I'll sit with arms wrapped around my knees, gazing down. I'll enjoy watching everything burn to the ground; I've hated the red house almost as long as I've hated him. I can feel it now, the heat rising.

~~LAST NIGHT~~

Last night, I clenched my fists together and whispered silently to a god I don't believe in, begging for a break, just this once: *Please, make him stick to beer.* Though unpredictable, more so with each additional can popped open, beer days are never the worst days.

He'd already finished one can and would certainly have another. I've lived with him long enough to know that. We can handle two or three, or even four. Problems start with the fifth beer, which too often leads to the sixth. Beyond six is…beyond hope. Still, any amount of beer is better than whiskey since whiskey days are the worst.

Because old habits are hard to break in times like this, I closed my eyes and prayed, hoping for the best. While chanting nonsense inside my head that no one else could hear, it suddenly dawned on me that I never really prayed in the first place. Not with any conviction. Praying is for people who don't know better. Praying is a luxury for those who don't have real problems. Praying is a waste of time for people like us. Our feet are stuck in the mud of the real world, a place where whispered prayers go unanswered.

Yet still I prayed. With all my might, hoping it would be different this time, I put my hands together and prayed.

Last night, when my father walked over to the kitchen cabinet and poured himself a cup of whiskey, I almost laughed thinking that maybe I just hadn't prayed hard enough. A bitter taste filled my mouth as I quietly retreated to the darkness of my bedroom. I didn't bother switching on the light.

Gazing out the window, I tried to see something beyond the deep black darkness that had fallen. I wondered why so many people believe in a supreme being who supposedly watches over us. If such a force exists, they must have a really sick sense of humor, watching us flounder and beg and pray while they do nothing to stop our suffering. If anything, they get off on mocking us, I figured.

That is, if they're paying any attention at all.

CHAPTER FIVE

Today is the day. This afternoon, to be exact.

I've already set the plan in motion, telling my father that I need help gathering mushrooms for my science class at school. Bringing them in for us to study will give me the extra credit I desperately need after missing more days than I can count. I'm always playing catchup with my classmates. When I asked about the mushrooms and explained why I needed them, he looked at me for the longest time before answering. Knowing my absences are *his* fault, not mine, he must have finally started feeling guilty about something. It's hard to imagine, but here we are.

It's not the first time he's shown signs of empathy. A couple of years ago, after one of our more difficult nights, he woke up early the next morning in an uncharacteristically good mood. He wanted to do something special for us, suggesting a drive out to a nearby mountain that's known for being the highest peak around these parts. My mother quickly agreed to go, managing a small smile, and I agreed as well, though it's not like I had a choice. I also didn't trust his supposed kindness for a second. I know better. As for my mother, specter that she is, floating through the house as quietly as a mouse, trying to remain as unobtrusive as possible, almost as if she thinks she can disappear if she focuses hard enough on not making a sound, even she had no real choice in the matter. If she wanted to maintain the peace of the morning, she had to agree to whatever he suggested. Prolonging the quiet times between the storms is all we can hope for in the little red house we call home.

In her bedroom, she searched for her sunglasses, and I offered to help find them. I call them her giant Jackie O. glasses. Smiling, she once asked what I know about Jackie O., and I answered, not much. Probably just something I saw on television. I pictured the dark-haired former first lady standing before the cameras, elegant and regal with her funny hat and giant sunglasses that shielded much of her face, like she needed a barrier between herself and the prying eyes of the world. Having faced such tragedy with her husband being shot and killed right in front of her, she had every right to hide whatever she needed to.

My mother, a simple woman who doesn't have the eyes of the world on her, longs to hide things as well. When she brings those giant sunglasses to her face, she does it with the same elegant grace as Jackie O. With her dark hair combed straight down, framing her face, and the sunglasses put perfectly in place, she's able to hide some of the things that she would rather no one see. The bruises she conceals are caused by other hands, unlike most of the ones I find across my own body. It seems only fair that I have bruises too.

We drove in silence, listening to sad, old country songs on the radio. My father quietly hummed along with the music, almost like a normal person. Passengers in other cars might have mistaken us for just another nice family out for a Sunday drive. Once we got as far as you can up the mountain by car, my father found a place to park. We had to walk the rest of the way to reach the summit, where the views are spectacular. Though I was enjoying myself, somewhat begrudgingly, I didn't want to give my father the satisfaction of seeing me happy, so I kept my head down and shrugged a lot, feigning indifference. Secretly, I loved the experience, walking around on a mountain so high we passed through thin strips of clouds on our way to the top. It was breathtaking.

This rare bit of joy didn't last long, however. It never does. It disappeared with the smoke from my father's cigarette, floating up, up, and away. I felt foolish when I turned around to find my mother struggling to catch her breath. At such a high altitude, people often get short of breath, but this was different. Though the elevation didn't help, she was having a difficult time because of her swollen, injured nose. I stared at her face, which was bruised and puffy, and worried her nose might be broken. The further we walked, the more she struggled. Finally, it became clear she couldn't make it to the top, so we stopped and turned around. Hanging his head down as we made our way back, my dad said very little, though he seemed to feel bad for what he'd done the night before.

This time, we'll drive up a different mountain, one that's not nearly as high as the one that caused my mother such difficulty. After hopping in the truck, I strap my seatbelt across my lap. If I left it unbuckled, he wouldn't say anything. He hardly ever wears his seatbelt, and this time is no exception. As I stare at the loose buckle beside him, an idea comes to mind—another possible way to end his life. But I turn away, deciding it's best to stick with the original plan.

We drive up the road from our house, my father with his cigarettes in tow, me with my plastic sandwich bags bunched up between my legs. They're for the mushrooms we're off to gather. I told him I know just the spot, discovered during one of my long bicycle rides. Just off the side of the road up near the dead end, there's a large patch of mushrooms growing. This part is true. But I have no real interest in collecting them. Blending a piece of truth with the lie helps make it more believable. I am cunning with my tricks, a true master of deception when I need to be. If some unforeseen obstacle arises, I can abort the mission and collect the mushrooms after all, even taking them to class for extra credit. Or I could just toss the mushrooms aside since it's not like my father will know the difference. He never asks about school, he isn't curious about my grades, and he's never shown any interest in how my day went. He doesn't ask me much of anything, really.

"We're almost there," I tell him, squirming around. The heat of anticipation has my palms slick with sweat, though I remain perfectly cool and calm, ready to do what I must. A surge of energy courses through my veins, feeding the power I never believed I possessed. The moment is almost upon us. I look down at my hands as I open and close them, slowly, assuring myself that they are ready—assuring myself that I am ready.

"Right there, right there." I point out a wide embankment for him to park the truck, telling him the mushrooms are up ahead, lining the steep slope that drops down just a few feet from the edge of the road. This quiet, isolated spot is the perfect place to kill a man. No one else is around, and few people drive all the way up here to the end of the road. I know since I've biked here so many times and hung around long enough to see its potential. About thirty feet ahead, the road just stops, marking the dead end. I've always thought there was something eerie about a road that stops so abruptly. It seems unnatural that it doesn't circle around or continue in some way, though I've come to appreciate this sense of finality, especially when it comes to putting an end to my father.

Barely able to contain myself, I hop out of the truck before he's killed the engine. I shut the door and scramble over to the narrowest part of the embankment, the part with the slope that suddenly drops off so steeply, making it dangerous if you're not careful. One misstep and down you go, tumbling through rough brush, branches sticking out, and all kinds of sharp rocks that could do major damage if you hit them wrong. There are so many, it's hard to imagine *not* hitting at least a few on the way down. Holding the plastic bags at my side, I turn around and look over at the truck. He takes his time getting out, lighting a cigarette as soon as he shuts his door. How fitting, I think. A cigarette before dying.

Without a care in the world, he takes a slow, casual look around. He has no idea what's about to happen. Leaning against the front of his truck, he crosses one leg over the other, glancing over at me for a moment. When I notice, he averts his gaze, turning to the trees lining the other side of the road. His face is blank, relaxed and at ease. He looks a little bored, like he's waiting for something to happen—almost like he wishes something would happen to make this day different from all the others. Or maybe that's just me. With the cigarette pinched between his thumb and forefinger, he takes a deep drag, completely unaware that he won't be leaving this place alive.

It's time to act.

I inch closer to the steep drop-off, pretending that I'm searching for mushrooms. Out of the corner of my eye, I see my father has turned his face even further to the side, away from me, focusing on something I can't see. Peering at him long enough to get a better look, I'm suddenly struck by the thought that I know so little about this man who is my father. Standing perfectly still and quiet as he smokes a cigarette, something about him looks old-fashioned and out of place. His rigid demeanor and tendency to gaze into the distance at something no one else can see makes me think of a cowboy out on some dusty old ranch. He's like the Marlboro Man, seen by millions but understood by few, embodying the idea of a very specific kind of guy—earthy and rugged and tied to the land in a way most modern men aren't. And though my father owns a few cowboy hats, he's not wearing one now; still, it's hard to shake this image of him as some lonesome cowboy who somehow got lost along the way, winding up far from everything he knows. Dressed in his usual faded blue jeans, old black t-shirt, and steel-toed boots, everything about him just seems wrong. It's hard to believe inscrutable men like him still exist, even here in the mountains of North Carolina. So many conflicted thoughts fill my head, swirling around as I try to reach a conclusion I can't quite grasp. I wonder if my father was always like this. If not, when did he change? What was he like before he met my mother, or before I was born? What was he like as a boy around my age? Did he ride his bike up streets like this, letting it drop near the side of the road as he wandered off into the woods, looking for tadpoles in the creek or a turtle he might bring home as a pet? Did he climb the mountain, higher and higher, just to see what he might find? Did he climb even higher still, just because he could?

It's hard to imagine my father as a boy like me, though I'm sure I've seen pictures of him taken during his youth. I try to shake it off, these rambling thoughts that circle back and forth, leading nowhere. There's no time for nonsense, I tell myself, squeezing my hands into fists. There's no room for mistakes. People die when you're not careful—the wrong people. I can't let this sudden burst of curiosity get in the way of my perfect plan.

I inch closer to the edge, pointing at some little white mushrooms. I call out, asking my father what kind they might be. He prides himself on his knowledge of the land—all that grows on it, and all that roams across it. He sighs loudly without answering but soon starts shifting around. Out of the corner of my eye, I watch him uncross his legs and stand up straight, taking one final drag off his cigarette before flicking it away and stomping it out. As he draws closer, I take a step back, moving off to the side so he can get a better look at the mushrooms. The closer he gets, the more I withdraw, though only a little at a time since I don't want him to suspect anything. I take a deep breath, I clear my head, I brace myself as he moves into place near me. To be effective, this maneuver must be perfectly timed. Closer, closer, he's now at the very edge of the embankment, leaning over to get a better look at the patch of mushrooms growing along the slope that drops off so suddenly before him. Any second and he'll bend down to get an even closer look, all while trying to maintain his balance—yes,

yes, here he goes, it's time! I take off, sprinting straight ahead. Before he knows what's happening, I slam into him with both hands, knocking him over. And there he goes, tumbling down the steep slope, and here I am, safe as I watch from above. This must be what he feels when he's looking down on me—powerful, mighty, in control. On his way down, he hits his head against a large rock—everything's happening so fast—he tumbles more, hitting everything before finally coming to an abrupt stop against a thick tree trunk. Slumped over with his limbs flung out at odd angles, he looks like a broken toy. I can't see his face, but I'm almost sure the back of his head is already damp with blood. His body must be broken and covered with so many bruises and wounds he'll never heal. Throwing my fist high into the air, I call out, loud and strong, disturbing the peace and quiet of the woods around me.

The guttural sound of my battle cry quickly fades into a small, distant echo. The silence that follows is so complete it startles me. There are no birds chirping in the trees, no insects buzzing in the bushes, no small animals scurrying across the dry leaves scattered all around. I can't even hear the sound of my own heart beating. I close my eyes, waiting, but there's nothing.

When I open my eyes, I stare down at the body. It doesn't move, it doesn't make a sound. I step closer to the edge of the slope, and closer still, never taking my eyes off him. Without thinking about it for a second longer, I scramble down the embankment, quick but careful. I have to be sure—I have to know it's really over. If he's still alive I'll have to finish the job. They might know it wasn't an accident…though it might be hard to prove anything definitively. Maybe, just maybe, they won't even try. Maybe I'll be luckier than I've ever been before.

No matter what happens, it's too late to worry about it now.

The world around me blurs for a moment, making me think all of this is a dream. When it comes back into focus, the back of my father's head is the only thing I can see. I consider giving him a good hard kick. I think of jumping as high as I can and landing on him forcefully with both feet, stomping until I've worn myself out. I could roll him over to have a good long look at his face before bashing it in: his eyes, his nose, his mouth and teeth—everything, destroyed. I want to smash him out of existence forever, just like he deserves.

But no, I don't need to turn him over, nor do I need to see his face right now. I don't need to see it ever again. Instead, I focus on the dark, wet hair that's normally combed so perfectly in place. Now it's a tangled mess, strewn with twigs and leaves and dirt. And the blood, there's so much of it. A part of me longs to reach down, to run my fingers through his hair, to feel the warm, sticky wetness of the blood. To know it's real, all of this. What I've just done, it's real. There's no turning back.

I won't touch him, though. Not unless I have to.

Taking one step back, and then another, I turn my head from side to side, hunting for a good place to get comfortable. As long as I can still see him, it doesn't really matter where. I pick a spot about halfway up the slope, near a tree curving out from the ground. After making my way up there, I settle down beside the tree, I hug my knees to my chest, and I wait, just in case the body moves.

We will never miss you.

~~CHAPTER SIX~~

Or, to ensure there's no room for error, I make slight adjustments to the plan.

Making him feel guilty over my school absences, getting him to agree to help me gather mushrooms for extra credit, and then having him drive me up the road to the spot I point out—that's all the same. Before broaching the subject with him, I bike up to the end of the road on my own. After verifying that the small patch of white mushrooms is exactly where I remember, I look around for a good-sized rock, hard and heavy enough to knock him out with one blow, but easy to grip in one hand. It doesn't take long to find the perfect rock. I try it out a few times, slamming it through the air. Satisfied that it'll work, I carefully place it off to the side of the narrow embankment so it'll be easy to grab. Just to be safe, I find another one, similar in size and weight. Again, I lift it up with one hand and bring it down quick, going through the motions of what I plan to do to him, my father. I practice a few times, pretending I'm bashing him across the back of the head and then watching him tumble down the steep slope, knocking against much larger rocks on the way down. I leave the second rock near the first, a little closer to the road. Now, I've given myself options, covering all bases.

And here we are, me looking down at the mushrooms, my father leaning against his truck, smoking a cigarette. Waiting long enough to make sure he's not looking, I snatch up the first rock, gripping it tightly in my hand. With the rock behind my back, I point down at the patch of mushrooms with my other hand, calling out to him. "Here's a lot of mushrooms," I say. "But I don't know what kind they are." I wait a few seconds, staring down at the embankment while keeping him in sight. So proud of his knowledge of the land, he thinks he knows more than anyone. I count on that. I planned for it. "Do you know what kind they are?"

It works, I've lured him over. In only a few steps, he's here, right before me, close enough to touch. I back up a little, but not too much. He's bending down, careful to keep his balance so he doesn't accidentally tumble down the slope as he tries to get a better look at the mushrooms. I pull my hand out from behind my back, leaving it at my side as I approach him with my quiet little cat feet. I grip the rock even tighter, satisfied that it's the perfect shape and size. I take a deep breath and brace myself, knowing I must strike the back of his head at just the right moment, in just the right spot. This initial blow is the most important. If I bash him hard enough the first time, I won't need to go in for more. Closer, closer, I remain focused on the back of his head and my need to see it wet with blood. Close enough to make it count, I hold the rock high, ready to bring it down as hard as I can.

***

Or, another variation.

The mushrooms, the drive up the mountain, the perfect-sized rock—still the same. This time, when I find the rock, I store it safely in my backpack. During the drive up, I keep the bag between my legs, leaving it unzipped so I can reach inside when the time is right. I don't buckle my seatbelt either. It could slow me down. I've explained where the mushrooms are and will point out where to park so he can keep his truck safe and out of the way. It's not like someone's going to come speeding around the corner and crash into his precious truck up at the very end of the road, but I know he won't want to take any chances. He's so proud of it, his sparkling black GMC. He waxes it regularly to maintain the shine. It's an older model that looks brand new because of all the work he's put into it. When he pumps the gas, pushing the truck to go faster and faster, it roars like a demon straight out of Hell. He holds the steering wheel tight, gripping it like a set of reins as he guides the truck around the curves of these old country roads. Anything standing in his way had better watch out.

The black GMC is his most prized possession, and I hate it. I hate its loud, monstrous roar, I hate the suffocating smell of gasoline when I ride inside with the windows down, I hate the threat of its overwhelming power vibrating against my small and useless body. The truck is part of him, the very manifestation of everything I hate about him. He rebuilt the engine with his own hands, piece by piece; sweat dripped down his brow, falling across those smooth metallic parts, and when he accidentally cut his hand, bright drops of his blood spilled too, making their way inside.

Thankfully, I don't find myself riding in his truck too often these days. When I was smaller, he made me hop in to join him for a trip to the gas station every now and then. Before getting out to fill the tank, he told me to go inside and pick out some candy, any kind I wanted, and a soda too. It was nice, this little treat. Something rare. Roaming the candy aisle, I felt overwhelmed by all the choices. Once he joined me inside, he always picked out a candy bar for himself, something with lots of chocolate; I usually settled on something fruity and chewy and sure to get stuck to my teeth. I had a sweet tooth just like him, though he seemed disappointed when I didn't pick a candy bar too. I liked chocolate but didn't want him to think we had anything in common.

An occasional treat of candy and soda at the gas station was the nicest thing my father ever did for me. But it'd never make up for everything else. Not in a million years. And I no longer care about sweets. He's the one who likes sweets, not me. And I will never be like him.

Instead of pushing him down the steep slope near the mushrooms, I'll take care of him here, inside the truck. The truck he loves so much. And he'll never see it coming. There will be many opportunities—when he's focused on parking ever so carefully on the side of the road, right after he kills the engine and turns to open the door, or when he's digging around for his cigarettes, pulling one out to light. This is war. This will be my surprise attack. I'll reach inside my bag, I'll grab the rock without him noticing, and I'll bash his head in, striking him again and again and again, screaming the whole time. No one will hear me. There won't be anyone around. No one but us. The first blow must be the best, the most fatal. I can see it now, I can feel it, the power in my hand wrapped around the rock, ready to go when the moment is just right. So he won't see it coming, it's best to start with the back of his head. But, any spot will do as long as I hit it hard enough.

Here we are, arriving at the dead end of the street. I point out the perfect place to park, just up ahead, right over there. Plenty of room for his precious truck; not too close to the hanging branches that might scratch his pristine paint job, yet enough out of the way to give any approaching vehicle ample space to turn back around. Annoyed, he furrows his brow and expels a heavy breath through his nose—it's a warning. How dare I tell him what to do. How dare I tell him anything. Who do I think I am?

Still, he heeds my advice, parking off to the side of the embankment, not far from the patch of mushrooms down the slope. The truck has eased into a stop, and now he's turning the engine off; its vibrations take a few moments to fully fade. It's time, I know it's time. Already the rock is in my hand, my fingers wrapped around it so tight it should hurt, but I feel nothing. He's reaching inside his pants pocket for a cigarette, his lighter. He's got it, the cigarette, it's dangling between his lips, he's lighting it—I'm lifting it, the rock, I'm holding on like I will never let go. I don't falter, not now, not ever again.

As he turns away, moving to open the door, I see my arm fly into action, slamming the sharp edge of the rock against his head with so much force even I'm surprised. The moment of impact elicits the sickest crunching noise I've ever heard as a large piece of his skull shatters and caves in, quickly followed by the sound of the driver's side window breaking as the other side of his head slams against it; I can see the spiderweb of cracks spreading across the tempered glass. I hit him again and again, harder and harder each time. The window gives more and more with each time his head smashes into it, finally collapsing like his skull, sending small shards everywhere. I keep going, I keep hitting, I keep smashing—at one point, I'm holding the rock with both hands, slamming it down with everything I've got. His head, his face is soon destroyed, but I can't stop until he's so bruised, bloodied, and broken that no one will ever recognize him again. Spurts of blood fly across the cab of the truck, streaking the windshield, covering the steering wheel, and splashing against my hands, my arms, my chest, my face. It's more blood than I've ever seen, but it's still not enough.

Somewhere along the way—I can't be sure of how much time has passed in the chaos of such a frenzied attack—I stop for a moment, just a moment, when I catch sight of what looks like a pinkish-grey worm, thick and wet, crawling along the dashboard. It's not a worm, I realize, and it's not moving. It's from him, my father; it's a piece of him, a slick, rubbery chunk of tissue from his brain, set loose and sent flying by the violence in my hands. I scream but I cannot hear it—I can't hear anything—and I keep going even though I know the job is done. I'm not sure how long this will take, but once I'm finally done bringing the rock down, there will be nothing left of him— nothing but a bloodied mound of raw flesh mixed with broken bones.

And then, I'll back off, I'll take a breath, I'll rest.

When I'm ready, I'll prop up what's left of his body against the seat before leaning over to start the engine. Then, I'll get out, taking the blood-stained rock and my backpack with me. On the driver's side, I'll reach across the body and put the truck in drive, steering the wheel towards the steep embankment. At the very last second, I'll slam the door and jump back, watching the truck go over the edge, tearing through thick brush and bumping over the jagged rocks until it crashes into a tree somewhere far below. His body will be tossed this way and that, all because he doesn't have his seatbelt on. If I'm lucky, he'll fly through the windshield. All the damage I've done will be explained by the devastation of the crash.

And it'll be over at last.

~~LAST NIGHT~~

Last night, as my mother and I cleaned the dishes at the kitchen sink, my father paced back and forth behind us, silently biding his time. Whenever one of his boots hit the floor in the living room, the heavy thump sent vibrations across the house that felt like a warning. At the sound of each step, my mother flinched beside me. Through the tension hanging over us like a dark cloud, I could feel her fear—I could feel her desperately clinging to the hope that things wouldn't get so bad, not this time. We deserved a break. But she should have known better. I should have known better, too. But there I was, feeling just as desperate as my mother, foolishly begging a god I don't believe in to spare us, just this once. *Please*, I mouthed silently, closing my eyes. *Not again*.

The sound of his boots stomping across the floor came to a sudden stop. We perked our ears up in nervous anticipation of what might come next. We knew something was about to happen. Something bad. It always did. The silence had to be filled, and he filled it like no one else. Though it was deathly quiet in those moments, I knew he was up to something, but I couldn't make myself turn around. When he flipped the television off minutes earlier, losing interest in whatever he was watching, we should have known the night was about to take a turn for the worse. He was after a different kind of entertainment.

For a while he stood as still as a statue, gazing at the blank television screen—or so I imagined. Maybe he wasn't looking at the television at all. Maybe he was looking out the window over the couch, wondering like I sometimes wonder what lies out there in the dark. Or maybe he was simply lost in thought, unsure of how the night should proceed—unsure of how *he* wanted the night to proceed. It's hard to tell when it comes to my father. Now that he had stopped pacing, time itself seemed to have ground to a halt. The entire world was holding its breath, all because of him. With a deep unease that bordered on terror, I pictured him staring at the backs of our heads, contemplating his next move. Thinking about how he might hurt us. My mother and I remained frozen in place for what felt like the longest time. Her hands submerged in the dishwater going cold, my hands clenched into fists hanging down. We couldn't turn around. That might set him off. To move at all required a strength we didn't possess. All we could do was wait.

And then, something happened. A stir, a quick shift of motion, the floor creaking behind us, followed by more movement, much faster—so fast we had no idea what it was at first. His ashtray, flying through the air, shattering the silence as it crashed against the cabinet, just barely missing my mother's head. Shards of glass exploded everywhere, and all I could think about were her eyes. It scared me, the idea that a single fragment of glass could leave her blinded forever. Gasping, she sank into a crouch beside me, covering her face with both hands before quickly turning to me, running her hands up and down my body to make sure I was ok. She searched my face, and I searched hers, each of us breathless. Each of us scared.

She was ok, I was ok. Both of us, ok.

But we weren't, of course. And we never would be.

CHAPTER SEVEN

I think of body parts, how bizarre they look under the right circumstances, especially when examined in isolation, detached from one another. There are parts of the body I'd rather not consider, ones we keep hidden. Some parts of the body can be wielded like a weapon, hurting others in the worst possible way.

Locked in the bathroom, I stare at myself in the mirror over the sink, examining each of my body parts closely. I return to my face, again and again, unable to take my eyes away for very long. I lean in closer, taking note of each imperfection. My skin is oily, there's a small pimple on my chin; there is no stubble to be seen, not a single dark hair sprouting anywhere. I wish I could grow a beard, a mustache—something to change the way I look, something to hide what I don't want to see. My slightly upturned nose, just like his; my high, prominent cheekbones, just like his; my large ears, just like his; my hazel eyes, just like his; the shape of my face, shaping up to be just like his. Everything I see is too similar to everything I hate. I look at this strange face that is my own and realize I hate it as much as I hate his. I long to transform this face into something else so I'll never see *him* in the mirror again. I pick up my knife from the counter, the one he gave me, hoping I'd turn out to be a different kind of boy, one more like him—I pick it up and run it along my cheek, wondering if I'm strong enough to press down just a little harder. Wondering if I'm brave enough to make that first incision, clean and precise like a surgeon. Wondering if I can detach myself from the boundaries that hold me in place, in one piece, but never safe—wondering if I can detach a flap of skin to see what lies beneath. Just a little pressure is all it would take. I want to see what's inside, though the idea of finding out terrifies me. If I cross that line, I don't know that I'll be able to return. I might lose control, flying into a frenzy of destruction, slashing and stabbing and hacking so fast that everything is ruined before the pain even starts to set in. My face, carved up beyond recognition, so grotesque no one will ever say I look like him again.

A drop of blood drips slowly down my cheek. I've pressed the knife too hard, forgetting how sharp I keep it. With great care, I place it on the counter, making sure it doesn't rattle. I tear off a couple sheets of toilet paper, fold them together, and press them against the small wound. The bright red blood seeps through the thin paper; a tiny wet dot at first, it expands out, changing shape as it grows. Fascinated, I can't stop looking at the odd shape of blood spreading out, little by little before finally coming to a stop. The paper sticks to my skin as I pull it off, but the flow of blood doesn't return. The small wound has clotted over. It's barely a scratch, and there is no pain. If nothing else, I suppose this has been good practice.

My father won't be so lucky.

In my dreams, I have a gun or a bat or a knife, yet nothing can stop him. In some of the dreams, I can't even depend on my own body. No matter how much I want it, I can't strike him, I can't stab him, I can't pull the trigger. I can't even walk. I'm crawling, just trying to get away from him. But he keeps coming, and I'm pulling myself along the cold kitchen floor, along the ground outside our red house, unable to reach safety. It's a scene that plays out over and over again, like a movie stuck on repeat. It's a circle going nowhere, a fate that's inescapable.

This is our life, this is my hell.

But I'm no longer sleeping, and my legs work just fine. My arms, my hands, my fingers—everything works like it's supposed to.

I leave the bathroom, pausing in the hallway to steal a glance into the living room. I don't even need to drug him. He's passed out on the couch, no chance of waking up anytime soon after last night. Last night, when he started with beer before moving to whiskey—before moving to other things. Out cold, he's spread across the couch, vulnerable and exposed. It's time, the perfect time. As I get closer, keeping the knife behind my back, I watch his chest rise, slowly, and then sink back down. Earlier, he was snoring. It infuriated me, the way he had the nerve to lie there, so cozy and comfortable, snoring away as if it was a morning like any other; the fury took hold, burning across my chest, finding a home deep inside my heart.

Dressed in nothing but a black t-shirt and loose, piss-stained white briefs, he has his arm bent over his face, shielding his eyes from the early morning light, making me think of a chicken fast asleep. You can force a chicken to sleep if you tuck its head beneath its wing and swing it around in a circle. It's a neat trick, one he showed me long ago.

He also showed me what happens when you snap a chicken's neck. I was surprised and horrified as we watched the poor thing flop around the yard, like it didn't yet know it was already dead.

I approach him, ready and unafraid. I think of what he's done. I think of what he did just last night. I grip the knife harder, ready to wield it as my chosen weapon. With my free hand, I gently pull the front of his briefs down, keeping my eyes on his face— he stirs a little but doesn't wake. He's exposed even more now. I stare down at the thick patch of dark, curly hair. Before I can think about it for even a second longer, I pull the knife out and lop his penis off with one quick, clean slice. It's much easier than I thought it would be, detaching it from his body. As I watch it roll down his leg and topple off the edge of the couch like a fat, rubbery noodle, he suddenly wakes with a scream, reaching for what is no longer there. His hands cover the gaping wound, trying to stop the blood as it bursts through his fingers, gushing down his legs, soaking the couch and dripping down onto the floor. His blood makes the red house redder still. He's screaming, but I can't hear a thing. His mouth is a wide-open black hole of pain. I think of picking the limp appendage up and shoving it inside that hole. I think of laughing at him, I think of telling him that this is what he gets, this is what he deserves— this is what's been coming all along. But I realize the job isn't done. I must finish it, I must deliver the final, fatal blow, burying my knife so deep inside him there will be no turning back. I do it, I thrust forward, sinking the knife into his stomach, pushing deeper, and deeper—as deep as I can. We haven't been this close in a long time. I can feel his warm, putrid breath against my cheek. I can feel him struggling against me, weakly. I can feel the moment he gives up, struggling no more.

~~CHAPTER EIGHT~~

Today is the day. It doesn't matter if I get away with it or not. I can't think of that. It's too distracting.

***

If I could take my hands and wrap them around his throat, squeezing with all my strength, watching him beg just as we have begged, would that be enough to get the job done? I see the blue veins at his temples bulging as he gasps for his last breath, flailing about before finally giving in. I must be there, up-close—I am there, feeling it in my fingertips, the precise moment the light fades from his hazel eyes, filled with regret for everything he's done.

***

I could take my baseball bat and bash his brains in. I keep it behind my bedroom door, easy to grab should I ever need it. It's always there, waiting, just in case things get so bad there's no time to think and I have to act fast. In the little red house, we're always on the edge of an emergency. Violence erupts when tempers flare—his temper.

Sometimes, in the deepest, darkest part of night, I snap awake, sweaty and scared. Sitting up, breathless, I can't be sure of what is real and what is not. There in the darkness, I'm still in that other place, the one inside my head. It's cold there, and so lonely. And it feels so real. There, I take the baseball bat in my hands because I have to. Because he keeps coming. Because he'll never stop. No matter how many times I swing the bat, I never hit him. I don't know why I can't make contact. Nothing makes sense as I swing and swing, missing him each time. Even when I grip the bat so hard it hurts, I can't make it work. I am small, I am weak. I keep swinging, and he keeps coming, undeterred by the weapon in my hands. Undaunted and unstoppable, he keeps coming for me. And I know he'll never stop.

He haunts my days, he haunts my nights. In my dreams, I should be free. But I'm not. I am nothing, I am no one.

Today, I'll take my bat and start swinging without mercy.

***

Or, another object could work. Anything hard and sturdy enough to do real damage. I once picked up a greasy frying pan when he was yelling at us. It just happened to be nearby on the stovetop, the only thing within reach that I could use to protect us. The grease left in the pan had hardened into a mushy white mess. Bits of cooked hamburger meat stuck out like little brown worms. I picked that pan up and aimed it like a weapon. I held it higher, hoping he knew I would use it if I had to. And it worked, in a way. He stopped, he took the time to look me up and down, carefully. Like he couldn't believe what he was seeing.

And then he laughed for the longest time.

***

It could be a hunting accident. He took me hunting once, and I hated it. I hated the sound of the dogs barking as they chased a squirrel up the tree, I hated the explosion of the gun when he shot that poor creature at the very last moment, after I refused. I hated the way he touched me, gripping my chin with his rough, calloused hand as he jerked my head around. *Look at it*, he said, forcing me to see what he had done. What he wanted me to do. I hated it even more when he pushed me down, pressing my hands into the warm, sticky blood. I have long hated all the ways he's tried to mold and shape me in his image, hoping I'll be more like him. That is, before he gave up. Now, when he's not yelling, he simply ignores my existence. Sometimes I wonder if I exist at all.

I could suggest another hunting trip, pretending to be interested this time, in the gun, in the hunt, in the kill. A bigger animal to track down, like a deer. Would he be proud of his boy growing into a man? Would he be hopeful that I'm like him after all? That I could still be the one thing he leaves behind, a little piece of him that lives on long after he's gone?

And then, in the darkness of the woods, I walk behind him, carrying my gun, but I've forgotten to put the safety on. He has warned me against it, but I am foolish, a foolish child. When I trip, the gun goes off, and there's nothing I can do to stop it. He's shot, he's down, and the warm blood trickles out. He's gone, just like that, all because of a hunting accident.

***

There he is, my father, passed out on the couch. After last night, there's no chance of him waking up anytime soon. Unlike me, who's wide-awake, who's been up all through the cold, lonely night, thinking. Shivering, shaking. Quietly pacing back and forth across my room, alone in the dark, listening and waiting.

There he is, vulnerable and exposed. I've already gathered what I need from the kitchen. A canister of lighter fluid, a box of matches. I'm so tired. Completely exhausted, yet I don't know if I'll ever be able to sleep again. There have been too many nights like this, followed by days spent in a haze. This, what I'm about to do, is the best way. I wonder if the heavy yellow curtains behind the couch will go up in flames too. I've always felt there's something sad about the couch, mostly because of the worn, faded cushions with the ugly floral design. It won't be missed if we have to get rid of it. Maybe we'll keep it after this is done. That is, if it survives the flames. I can already see the large, scorched spot across the cushions that bears the shape of his body. I wonder how burning flesh smells. Like meat frying? Like a pig sizzling over the fire?

Drawing closer to my father, I'm about to find out.

***

It's best to keep it simple. Today, I'm going to shoot him.

I know how to use a gun because of him. Any of the guns from his vast assortment. He insisted on teaching me even when I didn't want to learn. One shot is all it will take.

Once I've chosen the right gun, I must aim for the head and hold steady. I mustn't flinch when I place my finger on the trigger. I have to decide between a shotgun and a rifle, revolver or derringer. He carries his derringer everywhere, tucked into the inside pocket of his faded denim jacket. It's small and easy to conceal—and just as easy to retrieve. He keeps it loaded, ready to go. Ready to scare. Ready to keep us in our place, always.

It holds two bullets. One for me, one for Mom? I wonder.

I won't trick him with the tale of a wounded deer, nor will I lie about wanting to give hunting another go. I don't need to lure him outside and up into the woods where no one will see or hear what happens. There's no need to be fussy, there's no point in worrying about witnesses to my crime. I can do it here in the little red house we call home. This is the place where it all began, so it should be the place where it ends. His blood will splatter across the walls and soak into the floor. Everywhere I turn, all I see is red. When the police come, I can't imagine it will be a surprise, this thing I've done. They've been here before, called to the red house when we were so scared we didn't know what else to do. They must know something like this was bound to happen. This house, our house, has always been a crime scene in waiting. I might even get away with it. Because they know. They already know why.

I wonder how my mother will respond when it's done. I think of her, hiding somewhere, doing whatever it takes to make herself invisible. It's an inclination I understand. In so many ways, she's already gone. She's a ghost, floating across the floors of our red house, trying to drift by without being seen or heard. She has disappeared, and I think—I hope I can bring her back.

The sound of the gun going off might be enough. I see her flinching, I see her hand covering her mouth; I see her frozen in place for a few terrible moments, too terrified to come out. When she finally emerges, I see her eyes filling with tears, grateful I'm alive but horrified by what I've done.

I hope she understands. I will wait as long as it takes.

***

I don't need a weapon at all. It's better to use my hands, my bare hands. I'll gather my strength and jump on him like a wild animal, flinging myself through the air with one goal in mind: *kill, kill, kill!* I'll land on him with so much force he'll be stunned into submission. He won't have time to think, he won't have time to react, he won't have time to deflect my attack. Taken by surprise, he won't be able to protect himself.

I'm on him, reaching out to inflict the greatest pain possible. In the brown and green swirls of his eyes, he looks innocent for a moment, in a way someone else might look, someone who doesn't deserve this. For a moment, he looks like something I've never seen before—scared, bewildered, childlike. I wonder if, as a child, he was ever as scared as he is now. I wonder what he was like as a child. I wonder if he was— different. Against my better judgement, I consider withdrawing, but everything's happening so fast I barely have time to think at all. But then, there's a shift as he stares up at me, and I watch as that little spark of light inside his eyes is swallowed by the darkness. I see him for what he is, I feel the heat of *his* hate in my fingertips, so hot it might blister my skin. In his eyes, I can find no reason to spare him. I see nothing deserving of mercy. He has never showed us mercy, after all. Not even once. And now, neither will I.

Everything I need to know about my father lies in his cold, dark eyes. I want to erase it all. The pain, the past, today, and tomorrow—everything. I want to stomp it out of existence. I need to destroy it like it has destroyed me.

I'm still on him, remember? Like a wild animal baying at the moon, my transformation is complete. I'm straddling his chest, staring down at those eyes in search of something I'll never find. I'm screaming, I'm snarling as I plunge both thumbs down, forcing them deep inside the sockets until I hear the popping sound of two eyes bursting. It's wet and squishy, but I smash down harder, digging deeper, searching without finding. No matter how awful and warm and slick it feels—no matter how much his body shudders and spasms beneath mine—I keep going, digging inside his head with my thumbs, twisting and turning them around, smashing down as hard as I can until there's no life left. But then I take it further, going and going until I'm gone too. Until I've finally done it. Until I've erased us both.

***

It's time. You should already know how this will end. I've told you everything, in my own way. I've offered my confession.

Now, look at me, with eyes unblinking, and watch carefully. If you feel the need to look away, don't. It'll all be over soon.

I need a witness. I need a friend. I need someone to know how much it hurts.

LAST NIGHT

Last night, my father hit my mother. Again.

I got in the way. Again.

I got hit too, again. Mostly by accident. Mostly. For as long as I can remember, I've tried to protect my mother, even when it means getting hit myself. After being slapped across the face, after being bruised, bloodied, and broken, he has looked at me like it's my fault, enraged that I would dare get in his way. I look at my father and wonder what it means to be a man. I am still a boy, always wondering what it's like to be a man, always doubting I'll ever find out. I don't think he can tell me, I don't think he can show me. I don't think he knows how.

Last night, my father pulled his gun out and pointed it at my mother. Again. To show her who's in charge. To show both of us. To teach us a lesson we'll never forget. To keep us in our place. To remind us he controls everything, and we will not disobey. He uses the gun to make sure we know our lives do not belong to us, they belong to him. He decides what will happen. If we live, if we die. Yesterday, today, and tomorrow—it's his decision.

He pointed it at her, and I got in the way of that as well. It wasn't a brave act. It was desperate and stupid. I am stupid, but I never know what to do in times like this. I don't know what it takes to be a man. Standing between them, I could only hope he wouldn't shoot me, his only child. The son he always wanted, supposedly. It would be easier if he shot me than to watch him shoot her. That, I just couldn't take.

My father rages like a storm that can't be stopped, keeping the sky above our heads so dark we can see nothing else.

My father erupts like a tornado, ready to destroy everything in its path.

My father explodes like an earthquake beneath our feet, shaking the walls, tossing us this way and that, threatening to bring the little red house down once and for all. The aftershocks spread far and wide, making us afraid to let our guard down even for a second. We tiptoe through the house, wary and exhausted, convinced that the worst is still yet to come. We don't fully grasp the damage already done, nor do we feel capable of surviving another hit, no matter how big or small.

Last night was like so many other nights. He beat her, my mother. He hit me too, and, well, I know it wasn't an accident.

Later, he did…other things.

Again.

LAST CHAPTER

Last night, I decided that today will be the day I kill my father.

I've thought of this for so long I can think of nothing else, though I never wanted to be a murderer. Over the years, I've wanted to be so many other things: bag boy, mailman, biologist, teacher, lawyer, inventor, writer, doctor—something nice, something normal. Mostly, I just wanted to be free. It's what I've always wanted. To fall asleep at night, unafraid; to wake the next morning, just the same. I don't want to go to jail, I don't want to go to a special home, I don't want to succumb to whatever it is that happens to boys my age who kill their fathers. *Patricide.* It's a word I learned in school. *The boy committed* patricide, *which shocked everyone despite them knowing why.* I like it as a word, the way it sounds rolling off my tongue. I jotted it down in my notebook but almost immediately crossed it out; I wrote it again, and again, and again, crossing it out each time. To my classmates, *patricide* is nothing more than a vocabulary term to memorize, written beside the rest. A few letters strung together, meaningless beyond an upcoming test. No one at school will come to feel the weight of its meaning in their hands, burning through their entire body.

No one but me.

I think of the anger I've witnessed, the rage I've felt but never expressed, the fear and violence that's shaped me. I'm on fire with it, this demon-black thing crawling beneath my skin, burning me up from the inside out. To free myself, I must commit the ultimate act of violence. My only choice is to murder him, my father.

I've considered various ways to do it, planning the scene out in great detail to ensure nothing goes wrong. Thinking and thinking, making changes here and there, I've weighed the pros and cons of each plan. In my head, I've gone over the act a thousand times, playing out exactly how it will happen. But now, we're past all that. We've reached the point in the story where words no longer matter. It's time for me to make good on my promise—it's time to act.

I wish I had more time. I wish—many things. I'm so scared. Maybe more than I've ever been. My hands tremble, my heart races. The sound of my heartbeat is so loud I can't hear anything else. With each booming thud that echoes in my head, the world outside the little red house retreats further into the distance, fading into the fog until it finally disappears. The *thump, thump, thump* inside my chest is so intense I fear my heart is about to burst. If I'm going to do this, I must first calm down. All it takes is putting one foot in front of the other.

I take a deep breath, I steady my trembling hands, I tell myself that it's now or never before closing my eyes and counting to ten. *One, two, three, four…*ready or not, here I come.

I pick up the black hunting knife, the one I've been fidgeting with for the past few hours—the weapon he gave me. I unfold the blade that's extra, extra sharp. It's not a huge knife but it will get the job done. All I have to do is thrust it deep enough.

Out of my bedroom and into the hallway I go, making my way to the living room. Here he is, my father, passed out on the couch. He had a long night. We all had such a long, long night. So long I didn't think it would ever end—and it hasn't. Not really. It never ends. Life in the red house is one long, endless night, the darkness so thick and heavy it has us doubting we'll ever see the light again.

I can smell him from here, that sour scent of days-old sweat mixed with cigarette smoke, mixed with booze—mixed with something else that's mildly sweet. It's a scent I know all too well. He could never sneak up on me. In a room filled with hundreds of people, I could sniff him out, pinpointing exactly where he is without ever opening my eyes. His smell is something I'll never forget.

I draw closer, holding the knife behind my back as I approach his sleeping form. He has nothing on but his black t-shirt and loose, piss-stained white briefs. There's a hole in the armpit of his shirt exposing bone-white skin. I'm not sure he's ever been as vulnerable as he is now. I could do whatever I want to him—it's a power I've never known, one that he must feel all the time. With his arm up over his face, shielding his eyes, he suddenly starts snoring. I grip my knife tighter, enraged. He doesn't deserve to be so relaxed.

Staring at the large lump of his Adam's apple, I'm mesmerized; it juts out so prominently, like it's waiting to be sliced open. I remove the knife from behind my back and hold it over his thigh. Across his body I gaze, considering each piece of him carefully—his round, protruding gut, the lump of his exposed throat, the part of his chest that holds his heart. I wonder if his heart is beating as loudly as mine, especially in these final moments.

Thump-thump, thump-thump.

Like a ritual that must be followed, I take the knife and hold it in place over each part of him. His knee, his thigh, his heart, his face. Finally, I settle on his stomach. So soft, so easy. In and out, again and again, or so I imagine. I've never done something so brutal, so final. To be effective, my first strike must be good and strong and deep. This I know.

The knife hovers over my father's stomach in a hand that's no longer steady. It trembles ever so slightly. I wish I could make it stop. If only I could make it stop. Closing my eyes for a few moments, I listen to the explosion of my heart racing faster and faster. *Thump-thump, thump-thump, thump-thump.* Make it stop. If only I could make it stop. I grit my teeth, I tell myself: *Make... it... stop.* The pounding slows, just a little, and I take a moment to regain control.

I *am* in control—me. This time, I'm the one calling the shots.

Gathering all my energy to focus on slowing the speed of my racing heart, I feel more in control than I've ever been. And it works. My heart eases back to its regular rhythm. The throbbing sound of it beating like a slow and steady drum begins to fade into the distance—suddenly, it's gone. All is quiet in the room around me. The silence left behind is so deep it feels like I'm trapped under water with no hope of ever reaching the surface. I am surprisingly calm, and I know exactly what to do. The blood in my body flows like a river, leading me to the place where I belong. I only have to follow.

I see my hand holding the knife, I see the knife hovering over my father's belly, I see the blade turning towards his soft flesh. It feels like I'm far away, watching the events unfold. Watching it happen to someone else. The hand that is my own grips the knife harder, ready to plunge down. And then—and then, at the very last moment, I see another hand reaching out, holding steady beside the one with the knife. This other hand that must be mine turns over, palm-up, offering itself in a way I never planned. The hand holding the knife runs the blade over this other wrist, deep and hard, tearing the flesh open. Pain explodes and burns across my body as the blood pours out, spewing over the sleeping figure that is my father. The blood turns black as it soaks into his dark t-shirt.

I stare, astonished to find my answer in the blood.

He wakes with a start, confronting me with wide, bewildered eyes. He sees me clearly now. He hears me at last. He screams out, but I can hardly hear a thing. *What did you do?*

I fixed it. That's what I did. I made it stop.

He pushes me onto the couch that still holds the warmth of his body. It's wet now too, and warm with blood. My blood. A towel is wrapped around my wrist before he slips away to yank on his pants, his boots. He scoops me up in his arms, and I can't remember the last time he picked me up like this. I can't remember the last time he touched me at all, unless you count the hitting. I hear my mother screaming in the background and figure she's not a ghost after all. How funny—not a ghost. A ghost can't make noises like the ones she's making. At least, I don't think so. Maybe I'll find out, soon. Maybe I'm the ghost.

I don't feel so good. A little dizzy, a little faint. This is it, I think. The answer I've been waiting for. I can't talk, my throat is dry, my words are lost, but I want to tell him something, my father. Something important. He should know the only reason he's still alive is because we're so different from each other. I am different, after all; I am incapable of hurting anyone in the way he's hurt us. My pain—I won't spread it around like a coward. I've found a different way to be a man, all on my own.

Though, I guess I'm a liar. After spending so much time plotting the perfect murder, in the end, I couldn't do it. I couldn't kill my father. Something had to die today, however. Something, someone. A version of me that no one will ever get to see.

So many other things are flashing through my head, like the way the blood keeps coming. My body is stubborn, unleashing what can't be stopped. It makes me laugh. If only they could hear me.

My house is red, as red as the flow of blood from my body. My father's hands, they are red too. All because of me.

Carried outside, I stare up at the sky. It's so bright I have to close my eyes. The light seeps in anyway, but it's warm, it's nice. To be blinded by such brilliant light is an amazing thing. I'm going away now, just for a little while. I need to rest. I can feel it happening, my body relaxing, my body letting go as I fall back, settling into the current that will take me under, happier than I've ever been.